CASTELMEZZANO, THE WITCH IS DEAD

AN ITALIAN COZY MYSTERY

ADRIANA LICIO

The Home Travellers
Press

CASTELMEZZANO, THE WITCH IS DEAD
An Italian Cozy Mystery

Book 0 in the *The Homeswappers* series
By Adriana Licio

Edition I
Copyright 2020 © Adriana Licio

Cover by Wicked Smart Design
Editing by Alison Jack

To Jill and Robert
with whom we never met
but they are the perfect travellers
and perfect residents,
and mostly they taught us
the real spirit of homeswapping.

1

THE PATH OF THE SEVEN STONES

It was a glorious day. With a clear blue sky, fresh air, the yellow brooms in full bloom, it was the first sunny day after a whole week of cold and rain. Maybe the summer was finally arriving in Castelmezzano, a little village perched amongst fairy-tale rocky outcrops that looked more like Cappadocia than Southern Italy.

As the bees buzzed, the birds sang and the children played happily, one woman's mind was in a frenzy of rage. Concetta Natale Passolina – Etta to her family and friends – had just retired after 43 years of service at the Potenza School as an English teacher. She had been looking forward to this moment, but she had never imagined the Government would betray her so miserably.

The letter she had received from INPS – the Italian Institute for Pensions and Social Services – contained her projected payments for the years to come. If she had gone begging outside the church each Sunday, she'd probably have got more. She was hardly going to receive enough to survive on, after 40+ years' service as a faithful employee. She could count on the fingers of one hand the amount of times she'd been off sick – when she'd been pregnant with Maddalena, of course, and once more when she'd got the measles at the age of 45. But she had also worked numerous hours unpaid, she had loved her work so much.

Of course, had she still been married, she would have been fine. A couple could make an almost decent living out of two poor pensions, but she was alone. Her wedded bliss hadn't lasted for long.

Maddalena had been urging her for a while to sell her father's house, which was too large and too expensive for her to keep.

"See how much you spend on the heating alone?" Maddalena had scolded her mother innumerable times. As painful as it was, her outspoken child was right. And what now? Was she going to sell her family home or let it decay for lack of maintenance, adapting herself to live in one or two cold rooms and leaving the rest of the house to fall apart? Would she move to Granada and live with her tattooist daughter and naturopath son-in-law, when it was impossible for her and Maddalena to be in the same room without quarrelling? Even during the Christmas holidays, when they'd only been together for a week, they'd argued incessantly.

Living with a daughter who had such different views on life was not an option. Etta dreaded the thought of aging and losing her independence and autonomy, of being forced to go to live with Maddalena's family, or even worse, in a residence for the elderly. No, she'd have to exercise both her mind and body every single day, she thought, upping her pace and panting slightly as she felt her face turning the same colour as her red hair. She wouldn't move into a retirement home, not even at 90. She had always had to fight for everything in her life, and she'd fight to age with dignity too.

Following the old mule track connecting the village of Castelmezzano to Pietrapertosa, she had reached the Witches' Cave. She slowed down to push a huge pair of red glasses back up her slim nose and calm her breathing. She was nearing the old oak tree when she saw something whitish, half hidden in the overgrown grass.

She went closer. Was someone sleeping under the tree?

She took one more step. Was someone sleeping *naked* under the oak tree?

GOODNESS, WAS IT TRUE?

Dorotea Rosa Pepe – Dora to her family and friends – walked along Garibaldi Street in Pietrapertosa, trying to hide from the passers-by, and arrived at the hiking path at the bottom end of the village. She needed some time alone, and hopefully a little walk would soothe her hurt feelings.

The old mule track, fancily renamed the Path of the Seven Stones in an attempt to attract the more inquisitive tourists in summer, offered her what she wanted. She stopped at the stone fountain, drank a sip of the water. It was still as cold as ice; it had been a long winter. And winter had descended in her heart that morning, despite the June sun shining high in the sky. She had thought she'd celebrate her retirement from teaching, but a letter from INPS had made it clear beyond all doubt that there was very little to celebrate. After more than 40 years teaching French, she was being offered a pension that would hardly allow her to survive. From now on, she'd have to be even more careful about every single lira – or euro, as the currency was called these days – she spent.

She had looked forward to retirement, to finally being able to travel a little. She had no great ambitions; she was a simple woman who had never married, preferring to take good care of her father. A pity the man had maintained the ugly vice of gambling, otherwise Dora would now have had her own little house. But it had to be sold after her father's death to pay all the debts he'd left, which numbered more than a few.

Dora sighed. She held no grudge towards her dear father; no man is perfect. Stopping on the small stone bridge over the Caperrino River, one of her favourite spots along the walk, she

3

couldn't even take consolation from the beautiful day. She had imagined she'd be able to help Arturo, her affable nephew with an innate ability, despite his generous nature, to always land in trouble. But what could she offer him out of her meagre income once she had paid for the rent, bills and a little food?

Private lessons, she thought. Students still loved her, and if French was not as in vogue as it had been in the past, her English was still quite good, and she spoke a little German too. She could augment her miserable earnings that way, and maybe she'd find more sidelines to keep her afloat.

"No brooding," she repeated to herself as she gathered her energy for the climb up to Castelmezzano. Her chubby body wasn't as fit as she would have liked, but the daily walks would help. She tossed her head with determination, and her salt-and-pepper fringe parted in the middle, showing her red forehead, her face puffy from the effort. She passed the back of the Witches' Cave and strode towards the centuries-old oak tree.

Someone was on their knees, half hidden in the grass. Then the figure stood up and cried with all the power in their lungs:

"HELLLP. SOMEONE HELP ME. HELLLLP!"

2

THE WITCH IS DEAD

"Etta, is that you?" Dora cried, wondering what was happening. Could this woman, clearly beside herself, really be the strong, stubborn, firm teacher she had worked with for so many years?

"Help, help, help!"

Dora was concentrating so hard on her colleague that she almost stumbled over the naked body of a blonde woman lying just in front of her.

"She's dead!" Etta cried.

From the marble colour of the woman's shoulders and back, her stillness despite the volume of Etta's cries, Dora had no doubt her colleague was speaking the truth. She sat on the small wall and rummaged through her tiny pink shoulder bag, which kept her mobile phone and house keys safe during her scrambles. With trembling fingers, she took out her phone.

"112, how can I help?"

"We've found a woman at the Witches' Cave in Castelmezzano."

"Is she lost?"

"I... I... don't know," said Dora.

"Haven't you asked her?"

"Of course I haven't."

"Then I'd suggest you ask her first, and then call us back."

"But that's simply not possible."

"Madam, may I remind you that you are calling an emergency number and keeping the line busy for other citizens? We're not a chat line, nor an assistance service for lonely people."

Etta had been listening to her friend's side of the conversation, and she'd had enough. Stupidity always aroused a wild desire inside her to put things straight. She tore the phone from Dora's hands and spoke harshly.

"May I have your name," she shouted, "so I can report you for wasting valuable time?" She didn't wait for an answer. "We've found the corpse of a woman. She's dead. Do you want to send the carabinieri, or do you want to carry on with your moronic responses?"

This time, the man took Etta's name and address, and all the details of the two women's current position. He then asked them to stay put until the carabinieri arrived.

"And tell them to come on foot," said Etta. "It will take too long in a car."

The only carabinieri station was in Pietrapertosa, as the villages of Castelmezzano and Pietrapertosa weren't even 2km apart as the crow flies. But they were perched on the ridge of the same mountain range, the Piccole Dolomiti Lucane, and only the mule track connected them directly. The road had to detour 15km, and it was so windy that the journey would take a good half an hour, even for a car being driven as fast as many Italians assume they have to drive every time they get behind the steering wheel.

"Shall we turn her face up?" asked Dora. "Maybe she's not dead yet."

"I've touched her shoulder," said Etta. "She's far too cold to be alive."

Dora removed her coat and covered the beautiful ivory body – the only thing the dead woman was wearing was a scarf around her neck. Then they waited in silence, their eyes unable to leave the woman's silhouette beneath the coat.

"Do we know her?" Etta asked.

"You think she might be from one of our villages?"

"Why would she be here otherwise?"

"Maybe she's a tourist," tried Dora.

Etta shook her head, unconvinced. "With all the rain and cold of the past week and the Angel's Flight zip line closed, I don't think there are any tourists around at the moment."

With Pietrapertosa counting barely 1,000 souls and Castelmezzano 800, if a tourist had been visiting, the locals would have known straight away. The stranger's face would stand out from the familiar folk as starkly as a black sheep in a white flock.

"Who can she be, then?" Dora wondered, starting a mental list of all the blonde women she knew.

Etta looked around. "I think the morons are coming by car after all. It will take them ages to get here. In the meantime, we can make ourselves useful and have a look."

Dora nodded. It didn't take much to convince her to agree with whoever she was talking to.

"Who's going to turn her?" Etta asked. This time, Dora jumped back.

"Not me," she cried.

"Come on, you want to know who she is just as much as I do," Etta said, miffed. "Let's play morra."

They chanted together to three, oscillating their arms, then they threw their hands open and shouted a guess as to the sum of their extended fingers.

"Seven."

"Five."

As the sum was five, Dora won. It was Etta who had to turn the body.

It was more difficult than she had expected, as if the woman was determined to stay in exactly the position she'd been found.

7

When, sweating and a little scared, Etta finally managed to turn the body over, the two women let out a cry. It was one thing seeing a dead body lying face down, another thing completely to see the empty eyes and pained expression. And even worse was discovering that the body belongs – belonged – to someone they knew.

"Sibilla Petronio?" the two women said in unison.

They looked at each other in amazement. Sibilla was possibly the most beautiful woman in Castelmezzano. She had always been pretty, ever since she was a child, and still was, despite being closer to her 40s than her 30s.

"What happened to her?"

"She fell from the tree," Dora replied, looking at stone number 3 in the literary walk – a series of seven stones, from which the path takes its name, telling the tragic story of a young witch and her foolish husband. This stone resembled a couple of wings, and on the bottom it said 'The Flight'.

"Why would she have climbed the tree?"

"I don't know, but look." Dora pointed. A sturdy branch lay where it had fallen beside the woman.

"She climbed the oak tree – naked – and fell," Etta was now walking up and down, her thick fingers pointing out the objects she was mentioning one at a time. "Her scarf got caught on the branch, and if the fall didn't kill her, the scarf around her neck must have suffocated her."

Dora looked at Etta in admiration. She had always both feared and respected Etta, even though they were both teachers. Etta had lived in Germany for a few years, had a daughter, and, despite being divorced, had even managed to keep her family house. She represented everything that Dora wished she could have achieved in her life. Where Dora always sacrificed herself for someone else's good, Etta was an individual determined to walk through life in her own way. But rather than feeling jealous, Dora felt drawn to her, like an apprentice is drawn to a master of whatever skill they wish to practise.

A sudden question from Etta startled Dora from her musings.

"But we still haven't answered why Sibilla would climb a tree naked so early in the morning."

The two women's eyes locked.

"Because she's a witch," they said in unison.

3

RIDING THE WINDS, RIDING THE SEA...

E tta was searching the grass under the oak tree.

"There it is!" she cried triumphantly.

Dora joined her, looking where her friend's finger was pointing.

"Terracotta shards?"

"Exactly." Etta passed her hand over one of the fragments, bringing her fingers up to her nose. "Olive oil, mixed with herbs." Despite her sceptical attitude towards witchcraft, Etta, like any other villager, was familiar with all the folklore that went with it.

According to tradition, witches prepared a magic potion made of olive oil, preserved in a terracotta jar and hidden in the trunk of an olive or oak tree. On the nights of the full moon, it was said the witches would undress and massage the magic potion into their body, then pronounce the spell:

"Sottovoce, sottovento,

Sopra il noce di Benevento,"

(Riding the winds, riding the sea,

To the Benevento walnut tree),

...and fly in the sky to where all witches gathered to celebrate their Sabbath. Woe betide whoever emptied the jar, or worse broke it. The witch would instantly plummet from the sky and die at their feet.

A thought struck Dora. "So maybe she wasn't climbing the tree after all; maybe she fell during her flight."

"Poppycock!" The pragmatic Etta, of course, would not believe in magical flying of any sort, whether on a broomstick or otherwise.

"But you saw the jar, and she's naked, and from her shining skin I'd say she'd anointed her body with some unguent."

"That doesn't mean she could fly."

They were still looking at the vase, trying to forget about their cold and unresponsive companion.

"Look there," said Dora, pointing to one of the larger fragments of the broken jar.

Etta took it in her hands. On it was carved two initials: CS.

"S must stand for Sibilla, so what is the C for?" asked Etta.

"Maybe that's her witch's name."

Etta snorted. "Wouldn't Sibilla be enough?"

"Maybe not."

"Surely it's more likely to stand for Claudio." Dora looked blank for a moment, and Etta clarified, "Sibilla's husband."

Dora was nodding slowly and thoughtfully when, finally, they heard sirens approaching from up above. Etta put the terracotta shard back where she'd found it, and fewer than a couple of minutes later, the local carabinieri in their black uniforms joined them.

"Who made the call?" a lanky brigadiere in his thirties asked, his accent sounding suspiciously like it was from the north.

"We called," replied Etta, adjusting her glasses on her nose, more to establish her authority over the newcomers than because they had slipped out of place. "And I spoke to your operator. He's a moron…"

"So what's happened?" the brigadiere interrupted, equally determined to take charge.

Dora and Etta stood where they were and simply pointed to the body on the other side of the tree.

"Oh my God, is that a dead woman?" The brigadiere's small glasses jumped from his nose on to his lips. Readjusting them with trembling hands, he looked at the covered body and the long blonde hair framing the face that emerged from under the coat.

"What did the moron tell you, that we were inviting you for a picnic?" snapped Etta.

"What have you done to her?"

"What have *we* done?" Etta's green eyes seemed to pop out through her wide glasses. If looks could kill, they would have set the man on fire. "We found her, and thought it might be useful to raise the alarm. Were we wrong?"

"Of course not." The brigadiere had never seen a dead body in almost 10 years in the carabinieri. You don't stumble over cadavers if you keep moving from one sleepy village in the South to another, especially as some were so small, no one wanted to live in them.

Maresciallo Gaggio, a stocky man with a large belly, joined them at that moment. He was out of breath, and Dora wondered what state he'd have been in if he'd run all the way from Pietrapertosa.

He looked at the two women and greeted them. "Mrs Passolina, Miss Pepe, so you were the ones who found the body?"

Dora and Etta nodded at him, Etta smiling grimly.

"Marazzi, have you checked if she's dead?" asked the maresciallo.

"I was questioning the suspects..."

Maresciallo Gaggio looked around as if searching for someone. "Where are they?"

"These two women," Brigadiere Marazzi said sheepishly, by then knowing he'd made a mistake.

"Our teachers?" Gaggio dismissed him scornfully before

bending down to the corpse. "She's dead, and I know her identity. She's – she was Mrs Sibilla Petronio."

The brigadiere joined his superior, dropped to his knees and turned as pale as the fluffy clouds in the sky.

"What happened?" he asked, trying to hide his dismay.

"That's a bit more difficult to say," answered the maresciallo, struggling to his feet and looking around.

"And she's... she's..." the brigadiere tried to speak.

"She's what?" the maresciallo said briskly.

"Naked. Under that light coat, there's not a stitch on her."

"Really?"

The brigadiere nodded. "I fear someone may have abused her."

"That's for the pathologist to say. To me, it looks more like her scarf got entangled in a branch and she was strangled as she fell."

"Fell from where?"

"From the tree," answered the maresciallo, showing Marazzi the same branch the two women had noticed earlier.

"Or from the sky," whispered Dora.

"What?" cried the brigadiere.

"The sky," said Dora a little louder. "You know Sibilla was Castelmezzano's witch, like her grandmother and great grandmother. I believe the ability skipped her mother – Fortuna didn't have the gift."

"That's complete nonsense," the maresciallo said, his eyes widening with surprise at what he was hearing. "Miss Pepe, you're a teacher, you should know better than to spread rumours."

Dora flushed, and Etta shook her head in disapproval. But they were all missing the point. Yes, it was true Dora was a teacher, but she also knew everything about superstitions and beliefs, and she had a deep knowledge of the local area. Her grandmother, like all the older women, used to tell her tales after dark, sitting around a fire, and Dora was certain there were things that simply couldn't be explained by science… yet.

"You haven't touched anything else around here, have you?" the maresciallo asked.

"Of course not," Etta replied hurriedly, not giving Dora the opportunity to say something different.

"So when you arrived, everything was as we see it now?" the maresciallo continued, nodding pointedly towards the coat over the body.

"Oh well, the coat is ours. We thought we'd better cover her and preserve her dignity."

"And that's all you've done?" the carabiniere insisted.

"Exactly," lied Etta, more convinced with every passing second that they'd done something terribly wrong.

"So how did you know she was dead?"

"Well, I called out to her."

"She could have been in a deep sleep, or drugged."

"In actual fact," Etta admitted sheepishly, "I touched her, to make sure she was dead."

"How did you touch her?"

She had to acknowledge the battle was lost. As quickly as she could, Etta told the carabinieri how she had felt for Sibilla's pulse as she lay face down, then had touched her many times while turning her to face upwards.

"Mrs Passolina, you must be the only woman in the whole country who's not seen a police procedural on TV. Have you never heard of not interfering with the crime scene?"

"You think it's a crime?" Etta cried, a bit too enthusiastically. "It looks like a nasty accident…"

"We can't jump to conclusions. Anything else you touched around here?"

"The jar," Etta whispered, indicating the shards on the other side of the tree.

"Is there anything you *haven't* touched?" the maresciallo snapped.

"Nothing else, I swear."

"And we've been waiting here for such a long time," Dora blabbered, trying to sweeten the carabinieri up.

"You'd better disappear now, I think you've done enough damage for one day. I know where to find you if I need to ask you more questions. And we will probably need you to come over to the station so we can take your fingerprints."

Dora and Etta looked at each other, struck dumb with horror.

AS THE TWO WOMEN LEFT, THE BRIGADIERE TURNED TO HIS SUPERIOR.

"Do you suspect them?"

"Of course not."

"Then why do we need their fingerprints?"

"Use your brains, for goodness' sake!" The maresciallo missed his former brigadiere, who had been working with him for the past two years before moving back to Naples. He knew he'd have to be patient and teach this young man the tricks of the trade, but if the early signs were anything to go on, Brigadiere Marazzi didn't look promising at all. "If we have reason to suspect foul play, we need to see if there are any other fingerprints, besides the ones left – at their own admission – by those two meek and harmless teachers."

Brigadiere Marazzi nodded. In truth, he thought Mrs Passolina was anything but meek, but he prudently decided to keep his mouth shut.

4
_____

A LITTLE CHAT

Etta and Dora walked away from the Witches' Cave, taking the climbing path to Castelmezzano, uncertain what to do next.

"What a stuck-up moron," Etta growled. "After all, we found poor Sibilla."

"Do you think they're going to tell Claudio?"

"Sure they will. The poor man, to lose such a pretty wife. Why don't we go over to the main square? We've both had a shock, and sitting down with a cup of coffee may do us some good. Not to mention a chat about our eventful morning."

"Wouldn't we be better off in Pietrapertosa, then? After all, the carabinieri station is there."

"But the forensic scientists and the pathologist from Potenza will arrive in Castelmezzano. Access is better on this side, and they will surely take their coffee in the bar on the main square."

"Maybe you're right, but it's going to take some time for them to get here."

They climbed all the way up, passing the cemetery where the path started and pausing to look at the roses around the little pink Villa Chiara, the family home of the Petronios, set close to the inner road. But they couldn't enjoy the flowers for long as the municipal rubbish truck was rumbling past, collecting the waste.

"Would you mind if we stop at my place before trying to make sense of what happened?" asked Etta.

"Of course not."

Climbing through the tiny ochre alleys, enlivened by colourful geranium pots at the windows, the two women reached an old wooden door in an elegant stone frame that Etta opened with a large, heavy key. They ascended to the first floor and Dora was admitted into a large living room with a wood-beamed ceiling, terracotta floor and a terrace looking out towards the rest of the village, perched in amongst the fairy-tale chimney-like rock formations.

"I had forgotten how pretty your house is," said Dora, "and the view is spectacular."

Etta was proud of her house. She simply nodded, enjoying the look of admiration on Dora's face.

"Why don't you have geraniums and plants on the terrace?" Dora asked, peering through the window. "With very little, you could turn it into a sort of garden."

"I'm afraid I'd even kill plastic flowers," Etta admitted, opening the doors and following her friend out.

"Come on, it doesn't take much. You could have some roses climbing all around the door. Plenty of geraniums, which pretty much look after themselves; you just need to water them and cut away the dead flower heads."

"If only I could do gardening sporadically…"

What do you mean? Dora didn't speak out loud, but the question was clearly painted on her face.

"I can't bear the thought of having to do it every day. If only plants would be happy to be attended to once every quarter, then I wouldn't mind putting in some hard work for three to four days. But the silly things want water and care every other day, and weeding and fertiliser. No, I can't put up with that."

"I've no garden, but I fill my flat with plants anywhere there is a little space," sighed Dora. "Which doesn't amount to much. I'd be happy to help you."

"Then you'd have to come to Castelmezzano every other day!" Etta made it sound as though the two villages were 100km apart.

"I would be happy to do that," said Dora, smiling. "I mean, I've retired and I will have so much time on my hands now. I had already resolved to walk the Seven Stones Path every day for exercise."

"So that's what you were doing there so early this morning," Etta said. "The funny thing is not only have I retired too, but I was also planning to do the same thing. We can meet along the way every day, then."

"A pity we're starting from opposite ends of the path or we could have walked together."

"Yes, you're right. No one in Castelmezzano is interested in walking, then they complain about back pain and getting fat. But take a seat and I'll get our coffee."

With the smell of roasted coffee from the Moka pot filling the air, the two women sat on an ochre sofa and let the hot drink soothe their troubled feelings. It had been a grisly discovery. Putting her cup down on the low mahogany table in front of them, Dora recognised the white envelope with the light blue logo sitting there.

"That's from INPS, isn't it?"

"The bloodsuckers!" growled Etta. "They've been taking taxes and contributions from my meagre wages for decades, and now I've retired, they'll only give me just enough to eat and maybe pay one or two bills."

Dora shook her head sadly, understanding.

"The same for me. I was imagining that once I got to pension age, I'd be able to travel a bit. It's always been a dream of mine."

"Me too!" cried Etta emphatically. "With a little more time available and the opportunity of travelling off peak when the prices are lower, I fancied that I could finally get to see a little of

Europe – return to Germany, explore Scandinavia, visit the Cotswolds in England…"

Dora took up the theme with dreamy eyes. "The Scottish moors and lochs, the villages perched above Provence, Bohemia's castles…"

The two went on, naming places they had always wished to see. As the list grew longer, between a sigh and twinkle in the eyes, they could both see the places in their minds as they spoke the names. Then Etta shook her head gravely and articulated the harsh truth.

"But travelling is too expensive, and something a person on a teacher's pension can only dream of. Our best bet would be to follow Don Peppino on a pilgrimage to Medjugorje or Lourdes, singing Hallelujah with a coach load of horny 85-year-olds squeezing our bums every time we get off our seats."

Dora laughed heartily. "At least you have a pretty house to take care of. You have space for all your books, a charming kitchen to cook in."

"I can't cook."

"You'll have all the time in the world to learn now."

"I'd almost prefer a trip with Don Peppino."

"And you could adopt a stray cat…"

"Never!"

"Why not? I used to have a she-cat when my dad was alive," and Dora's eyes went watery all of a sudden. "Carinzia was such sweet company for me, a lovely pussy…"

"I'm sorry, Dora, but I believe dogs and cats are meant to be animals and be treated as such. I can't understand all this affection bestowed on them, nor people treating them like humans. If God had meant it to be that way, He'd have created more humans, not smelly, hairy things."

But Dora's thoughts were on her pretty tabby cat, and she didn't listen to anything Etta was saying.

"Anyway," she said, sending a silent prayer up to her sadly missed furry friend, "I don't think it needs to be that expensive."

"Keeping cats?"

"No, travelling. The sister of a friend of my cousin, Federica – actually, the wife of Dr Spaccaossi, the orthopaedic doctor – says she and her family travel the whole world on a budget by using home exchange. And there are four of them – the couple have two girls. They've been doing this since the children were babies."

"Home exchange? What devilry is that?"

"You know, you go and stay in someone's home, and they stay in yours."

If the floor had just collapsed beneath Etta's feet, she wouldn't have panicked as much as she did at Dora's words.

"You mean, a stranger – actually, a whole family of strangers, perhaps with pestiferous teenagers or a poopy baby – stays in *my* house?"

"Exactly," Dora said, clasping her hands together with a dreamy expression on her face. "And you'd stay in theirs rather than some anonymous hotel. A real house, away from the tourist traps, sharing the authentic lives of normal people."

"That sounds like one of those devilish New Age things. I hope Maddalena never hears of it. You'd end up in trouble, hosting God knows who and coming home to find your house emptied and vandalised."

"In thirty years of home swaps, Mrs Spaccaossi has never had a bad experience. Her husband earns quite a lot of money, but she can't imagine enjoying any other way of travelling as much…"

"They must be a stingy pair if they deny themselves a decent hotel in favour of handing their home over to any pervert who comes along."

"They do nothing of the sort. They subscribe to the Home Swapping Circle International, check the house photos and the family's profile, then write and get to know each other…"

"And I guess they all have splendid villas with swimming pools, except when you get there you find out that's the neighbours' house, and your holiday home is some musty basement you'll have to share with rats and beetles."

"If that were the case, the club would throw the people out immediately. You can't cheat, because the moment you walk into someone else's house, they're also walking into yours. It's all about sharing and respect. And Mrs Spaccaossi said they have become friends with a lot of the people they swap with and they're still in touch years later."

"You're so well informed," Etta said suspiciously. "Are you already a member of the Home Swapping whatever?"

"I wish. But my house is a plain two-room effort in one of the only two ugly buildings in the whole of Pietrapertosa. Also I'm sure my landlord would never allow me to join such a scheme and have guests at my place."

"I might be joining you sooner than you think," sighed Etta, dropping her head into her hands.

"What are you saying?"

"Keeping a house *this* big with *this* pension," Etta agitated the INPS letter in the air before flinging it back on the table, "is an impossible challenge. But enough, or I'll need to pay for high blood pressure pills too. That's why I was out for a walk today – I need to stay healthy and fit for as long as I can. But I hope I'm not going to stumble across a corpse every time I do some exercise."

Dora looked at her, horrified. "Certainly not."

"Still, I wonder what happened to her. To Sibilla, I mean. Did she die in the middle of the night? What was she doing there?"

"It must have been to cast one of her spells. Yesterday was a full moon..."

"How do you know?"

"About the spells?"

"No, about the moon!"

"I looked out of my window."

"I also look out of my window," Etta said impatiently, "but

like most people, I don't take any notice of whether the moon is crescent, waning or whatever."

"That's because you're not a gardener."

"Don't tell me you look at moon phases for your Ficus Benjamina?"

"No, for the seedlings in my pot vegetable garden."

"I see," said Etta, quite impressed, but trying not to show it. Instead, she looked through the door at her noisy pendulum clock. "Shall we go downtown and find out what's happening?"

5

MUNDANE GOSSIP

W alking down the alley, Dora and Etta reached Piazza
Emilio Caizzo, Castelmezzano's main square sitting just
below the stone church of Santa Maria dell'Olmo and continuing
in an airy terrace that offered a superb view over the village
perched on the Little Dolomites, the houses' façades suspended
above the void and the strangely shaped rocks. They knew that if
they wanted to hear local news in Castelmezzano, they could
wait for the TGR – the regional TV broadcast – or they could surf
the web, but first-hand information could only be found in the
main square around midday. That's when the older women
would be going to church for a little prayer and to offer flowers
to the Madonna; housewives would visit the mini market for
their daily shopping; farmers, bricklayers and other workers
would take a break in the local bar. But there was a precise
moment when all these folks would stop their errands, finish
their coffees, kiss the Madonna's feet, and congregate at the same
time, as if called by an invisible horn, in the main square. There,
terabits of information were available via the fastest and most
ancient of wi-fi systems: gossip.

When Dora and Etta arrived, they could tell something odd
was going on. Not only had the usual number of people in the

square multiplied, but the buzz hovering over them was almost as loud as in the centre of a beehive.

Etta dragged Dora through the multitude of little groups populating the square until she reached the one containing Costanza Di Vitello. Costanza was not only the best butcher in town, she was not only sharp tongued and outspoken, but she was also Maresciallo Gaggio's sister. If there was anyone there with authentic first-hand information, it was she.

A huge, imposing woman, Costanza was as tall as she was wide. She had tried to tame her frizzy brown hair in a knot, but her bangs had escaped the black elastic band holding them. Two vertical lines separated eyes as scary as lightning bolts in her red face, giving the impression she was permanently angry with whoever was in front of her, whether it be human, beast or inanimate object. Etta wasn't as tall, or as wide, but she had the same voluminous ego. Saying that the two women could not stand each other was an understatement.

Costanza looked at Etta fiercely. Etta glared back just as ferociously. The eyes around them darted from one to the other, wondering if another corpse was going to accompany Sibilla's in the morgue, only this time they'd be lucky enough to be eye witnesses. But the news was equally exciting, and if Costanza had the carabinieri's version of events, Etta had been the one who had actually found the body. A glance settled the matter: a truce was silently agreed.

"Good morning, Mrs Passolina," Costanza said in a growl, which was a sign of acceptance from her.

"Good morning, Mrs Di Vitello, I guess you've heard the news. Miss Pepe and I happened to be..."

And Etta told all she and Dora had seen. Costanza nodded, greedily taking in all the details her brother had left out during their brief phone conversation: the way the body had been found, the terracotta jar and the olive oil, the scarf, the anointed skin.

"Miss Pepe suggested," Etta continued, "that yesterday was a full moon and maybe Sibilla was out casting her spells. I was wondering if the carabinieri have found out when exactly the accident happened. Have they any hypotheses yet?"

"Accident?" cried Costanza, her eyes widening like those of an ogre ready to eat his human prey. "There was no accident whatsoever. Sibilla was killed, strangled with a rope, and then the murderer tried to pass it off as an accident, as if she'd fallen out of the sky to land next to the oak tree from where the witches are supposed to fly."

A chorus of "Oooooh" rose from the crowd. Don Peppino would have been proud to have them in his choir, so synchronised and harmonised were their voices.

"When did this happen?" Etta asked without missing a beat, as if she had known all along that it was a murder case.

"Around two o'clock this morning, the pathologist said."

"The poor husband."

"Poor bollocks!" Costanza snapped. "Claudio and Sibilla didn't get on at all. I often heard them squabbling and bickering savagely in my shop."

"If we were to assume every quarrelling couple is likely to kill each other," said Etta dismissively, "we'd only have one or two people left in the village."

The folk around nodded in approval, many thinking of their own belligerent partner.

"What you're obviously ignoring," snarled Costanza, "is that Claudio Petronio navigates in rather turbulent waters."

"He's got a profitable company. That must make up for his occasional folly." Etta said this more as provocation than because she believed it. And the bulk of Costanza fell right into her trap.

"I don't think so, my dear preachy teacher. Neither his preserve business nor his estate agency has been making money for the past few years. The man has accumulated debts with banks, suppliers, sharks, employees, and he would also owe the local shops if it weren't for Sibilla paying all the family bills."

Spectators clapped their hands; this was big news indeed.

Claudio Petronio, with his pompous mannerisms and proud statements, had never been suspected of being short of money. His employees had often complained about their wages coming in fits and starts – more fits than starts – but they thought it was due to a combination of his erratic investment projects and difficulties in the market.

"Really?" asked Etta.

"Really."

"Are you telling us he might have killed his wife?"

"I didn't say that. But when the carabinieri went to look for him, he was nowhere to be found, neither at home nor at his office."

"But why would he kill his wife?" gasped Dora, daring to put her beak into the duel for the first time.

"For the oldest reason in the world…"

"Money?" the people around them chorused.

"Exactly." Costanza nodded, sending a triumphant look over the huge crowd that was now gathered around her, hanging on her every word. "Sibilla had money from her family. But she knew Claudio's flaws and vices, and even at the beginning of their marriage, when they were still in love with each other, she insisted on the condition that their money would remain separate. As an only child, she inherited all the money her father left when he died. Maybe she wasn't rich, but she was surely better off than her husband."

"And she owned a couple of houses in Potenza that she rented out," an old woman with a missing incisor blurted.

"And didn't she help her husband?" another woman, wearing a black scarf around her head, asked.

"No. Maybe she did at the beginning," Constanza snorted like an enraged bull, "but she soon realised that the more money she gave him, the more he'd squander. So she paid for their food and bills, but she kept him far away from her money."

"Why didn't she divorce him?" asked a 40-year-old man,

known as much for his laziness as his unorthodox views on family life.

"Oh no, she'd never do that," said Constanza, lowering her voice for the first time.

"For religious reasons, you mean?" Etta asked.

"No, I don't think so…"

"Then why? As you said, they were renowned for quarrelling and fighting ferociously…"

"If you ask me," Constanza clearly felt everyone should ask her, "and it's only my humble opinion, but I believe that Sibilla was still in love with Claudio. She knew he was ruining their lives, and she was mad at him for that so she freaked out every now and then. She *threatened* to leave him, making sure he would never get his hands on her money, but no, I don't think she would ever have done it."

Was there a catch in Constanza's voice? Nobody had ever known her to show any weakness, so when she plucked a tissue out of her pocket and wiped her eyes, then blew her nose loudly, people were shocked. The indomitable bull had a heart, after all.

It took a long moment before folks started talking again. Then there were more comments, more rumours, more memories of things that had really happened and even more of things that never had. Finally, when the clock chimed one, everyone remembered that as big a tragedy as Sibilla's passing was, an even greater tragedy would befall their households if lunch wasn't served on time.

As the main square emptied, Etta asked Dora to stay for lunch.

"I have a frozen minestrone in the freezer."

Dora accepted the offer, but stopped briefly at the mini market, saying she'd take care of the food. And back at the house, when the delicious aromas reached Etta's nostrils from the kitchen, she realised Dora had a different plan for lunch altogether. Dora served penne with rucola, tomatoes and speck, and it was simply delicious.

"I really can't cook," admitted Etta.

"It doesn't take much time nor effort, and it's good to eat fresh food instead of frozen or microwaved stuff."

Etta nodded, but culinary skills simply eluded her. She'd stop in the middle of preparing a meal to go and read a book, or watch a TV programme, and by the time she got back, it had invariably burned. Or she'd swap one ingredient for another, only to find out the substitution didn't work at all. Not to mention the fact that, in order to cook, she'd have to plan in advance and go shopping accordingly. The fresher the food, the more often she'd have to go shopping. With frozen stuff, she only needed to go to the supermarket once a month and she was done.

But the juicy penne was just perfect.

"I'll do the dishes," Etta offered in gratitude after they'd eaten. But as they chatted some more, sitting on the living room sofas, before they knew it, their heads had drooped and a gentle snoring filled the room.

6

OF SPELLS AND WITCHCRAFT

After the nap, Dora and Etta shared memories of their years as school teachers, moving on to people in the village, the importance of keeping fit and how they'd meet every other day along the path to do some hiking together or visit nearby villages. For the first time since they'd realised their retirement was coming closer and closer, they felt that maybe it wasn't necessarily the beginning of endless days watching the hours slowly ticking by.

Etta offered to drive Dora home, but Dora refused. "It would take a whole hour to do the round trip, and I still need to do my walking."

In the end, they decided Etta would accompany Dora as far as the Witches' Cave so she wouldn't have to face the place alone. The carabinieri had gone, but a tape was cordoning off the area. The women assumed the carabinieri would return to do further searches, although surely they had gathered most of the evidence they were going to find already.

They parted and Dora continued along the Caperrino River, passing the old stone bridge and climbing up the steep path. It had been a wonderful day. Etta's home seemed to her like a mansion, or maybe even a castle. The large rooms, the high ceilings, the well-equipped kitchen – the only problem now was it made the prospect of returning to her ugly, dingy flat more unattractive than it usually was. She was even denied the benefits of a view, since her window was overlooked by a bulky modern building.

The sunset was finally drawing in, and before long, the evening would take over. The sky was an intense shade of blue, the swallows were loud and frenzied in their flight. Before she knew what was happening, Dora's feet were taking her towards the Convent of Saint Francesco rather than turning left to her flat. From the convent, she could look out over the whole valley. And daydreaming came so easily at sunset.

DORA WAS AWOKEN FROM HER THOUGHTS BY VOICES COMING FROM the carabinieri station, just a stone's throw away. She recognised Claudio Petronio's tall smartly dressed figure, accompanied by his sister Agrippina, small and angular. They were walking along the pavement in her direction, and some inexplicable instinct made Dora hide behind one of the columns of the convent's front porch.

Agrippina was clearly trying to cheer her brother up. "Everything will be fine, don't you worry," she was saying when a figure shrouded in a dark cloak leapt out from behind the monument to the Second World War victims and confronted the two of them.

"You obnoxious killer," the cloaked figure shouted in Claudio's face, "you will pay for your evil deeds. You took away my sister's life, and you will regret it.

"Dirididaradan, peace and quiet leave the man;
Dirididaradoon, dark and fear be his doom."

And with that, the dark shape cupped her hands in front of her lips and blew a dark powder all over the man's face. Claudio choked as his sister screamed, then bent down to pick up a stone and throw it at the witch, who was slipping along the alley as fast as a wild cat. She cried out as the stone hit her and turned, her fist pointing to the sky.

"Hell is waiting for you too!" And with a sinister laugh, she disappeared into the shadows of the darkening alley.

"Oh my goodness, what are we going to do now?" Claudio said.

"Absolutely nothing. That stupid witch has something to hide." Agrippina's sharp face contorted as she let out a loud laugh, her voice sounding even more sinister than that of the witch.

Brother and sister entered a black car parked close to the convent. As they sped off and disappeared from view, Dora flew home. This time, she didn't mind the weathered main door, nor how small her living room was. She sat on a chair and called Etta to tell her what she had just witnessed.

"Do you think it was Cassandra who confronted them?" Etta asked her.

"Who else? She's the only witch in Pietrapertosa."

"But if the carabinieri released Claudio, it means they are not convinced he's the murderer…"

"Maybe they have no proof."

"Maybe."

"Or they might be waiting for the forensic results. They might arrest him tomorrow, for all we know…"

"But why would he kill her in such a dramatic way?"

"What do you mean?"

"Sibilla was found naked in front of the Witches' Cave. Then there's the olive oil, the jar, the tree…"

Dora considered the question. "What about the flight?" she cried. "All the pieces combine."

"I'm afraid I don't see what you mean."

"Do you know the story of *Vito and the Witch*?"

"I might have heard of it when I was a child," said Etta, annoyed that she couldn't remember the details.

"Vito was a farmer," Dora began. Her enthusiasm never failed her when it came to telling a traditional story. "One night, he woke up and, to his horror, discovered his beautiful wife naked, massaging her body with olive oil from a terracotta jar and reciting a spell. She then flew off to meet the other witches at the Benevento walnut tree, and that's how he got to know what the mysterious woman he had fallen in love with truly was."

"So we have the jar, the oil and the naked body..."

"Don't you remember how the story ends?"

"Nope."

"Vito was mad at his wife for having lied to him – she had never told him she was a witch. One night, he pretended to be asleep, but as his wife flew away, he broke the jar containing the magic oil. At that very moment, his wife fell from the sky and landed at his feet. With her dying breath, she told him she had always dearly loved him. And the man, desperate and broken hearted, still wanders through our forests and woods, crying for his lost love..."

Despite her natural scepticism, Etta felt a little shaken by the story she hadn't heard since she was a child. As Dora fell silent, she remembered her granny telling her the tale as they sat around the fireplace during the winter nights, a long time ago.

"I can't see how Vito is relevant to our present case."

"It's simple. Claudio must have seen his wife going out in the middle of the night and followed her to the Witches' Cave. She got undressed, massaged in the oil, and then flew away. Claudio, angry that his wife was a witch, must have thrown the jar containing the potion to the ground. Instantly, the jar broke, and poor Sibilla fell from the sky. Her scarf got entangled on a tree branch and strangled her before the branch broke and she hit the ground."

"As I have already reminded you," Etta snapped, "people can't fly unless they're on an aeroplane."

"But can't you see? That's why the carabinieri couldn't arrest Claudio. They can't send him to jail as he has only broken a jar.

But Cassandra knows how things are and she wants to avenge her witch sister."

"Dorotea Rosa Pepe, that's a lot of balderdash. Let's wait and see what tomorrow brings."

But when she went to sleep, Etta dreamed of wild burning eyes looking at her fiercely. As her gran always used to tell her, witches have a fire inside. And she saw a desperate man running feverishly through the brambles and thorny vegetation of the woodland in the throes of madness over his lost love.

7

THE HUSBAND WAS AWAY

O nce she had completed her morning routine and she finally sat down to read the news, Etta found to her surprise that she was simply unable to concentrate. And not only that, she felt an urgent need to call Dora; it felt so good to have someone to chat with. She tried to ignore the feeling, bending close to the newspaper to read some more, but her eyes just scanned the words mechanically while her mind... well, her mind was on the dead witch and what Dora had witnessed the previous day.

She put the newspaper back on the small reading table and picked up the phone.

"Dora?"

"Etta, I'm so glad you called. I was wondering whether to disturb you."

"About what?"

"The whole night, I've been thinking of poor Sibilla, and Cassandra being so heartbroken. I might go to visit her and cheer her up. In fact, I'm baking some brioches with saffron and orange peel to take with me."

"That sounds like a good idea, there's nothing like first-hand information. You can ask her if she knows why Claudio wished his wife dead, apart from his financial troubles, I mean. Maybe there's a more sinister reason."

"I'm not sure she will tell me much, she's quite a taciturn type, but I'm glad you approve. I will call you back later."

"Yes, and in the meantime, I think I'll go to visit Claudio."

"But it might be dangerous as things are..."

"No, mine will be strictly a business visit."

Dora wanted to know more, but Etta was tight lipped. She had hardly put the receiver back in its cradle before she was searching for Claudio's number in the phone book.

It was Agrippina who answered, her voice hard and annoyed.

"Mrs Petronio, I'd like to speak to your brother..."

"This morning, everyone in Castelmezzano wants to speak to him. Don't you understand what a huge blow this has been for him? My sister-in-law has been killed and we don't want gossips sticking their noses in; we want to be left alone to grieve by ourselves."

"I understand it is an awful time for you, and I must seem selfish, but I was actually calling about my house. I'm determined to sell, but I realise now it might be an inopportune moment to talk business..."

"But Mrs Passolina, that's an altogether different kettle of fish. My apologies for having thought you were just another gossip. If you're calling about your beautiful house, then I'm sure my brother will have a minute to spare for you. After all, life must go on."

And with that, not only did Etta manage to speak with Claudio, she was also invited to visit him at his home. Within 15 minutes, she was ringing his doorbell.

"I'm so glad you called, Mrs Passolina," Agrippina said, inviting her in. She was a small, bony woman, her dyed black hair and her white skin a ghastly combination. "You see, it's such a hard time for my brother. It might do him some good to do something constructive and take his mind off it. He's always been passionate about his job. Please come along," and she guided Etta through a long, dark corridor of the type popular in the 70s before open plan came into fashion.

Claudio was sitting in the living room. He dropped the newspaper he had been reading with an elegant flick of the wrist and stood up to greet her with a sad smile.

"I'm so sorry," said Etta, for the first time wondering if she wasn't just another nosey old biddy preying on a poor, innocent victim.

"It's an awful time, Mrs Passolina. My wife and I have gone through our fair share of ups and downs, I won't deny it..." He had to interrupt himself as tears filled his eyes. A portrait of Sibilla on the chest of drawers behind him revealed how pretty the woman had been. "But when you lose someone so special, that's when you put everything into perspective and understand what's most important in life."

Beside the portrait was another frame with a letter inside. In a spiky, almost illegible script, similar to Etta's own handwriting, was a short poem to a dear husband. Claudio intercepted her look and nodded, suffocating a sob as if to say, *"Yes, these are the things that really matter, not the occasional quarrels we had."*

"I only hope they catch the brute." The silent conversation was interrupted by Agrippina reappearing in the room with a heavy silver tray carrying a large Moka pot and coffee cups.

"Do you have any suspicions?" Etta asked.

"Indeed, Mrs Passolina," said Claudio, sighing heavily but evidently recovering from his moment of weakness. "I have a clear idea, but I'm not going to share it with anyone but the carabinieri. I wouldn't like to point someone out as a suspect only to discover they're innocent."

"Yes," Agrippina added, "we're aware of how venomous the gossips in this village are. I wish Domizio my husband – I'm sure you've met him – were here with us. I'd love to see how many people would dare gossip then..."

Etta's mind went quickly to the few times she'd encountered

Domizio. Hardly the most intelligent being ever, to put it mildly, he was certainly a muscular brute of a man. But for reasons lost in the unpredictable chemical reactions of love and desire, he was completely and irremediably wrapped around Agrippina's little finger.

Luckily, Agrippina could not read people's minds, particularly not the astute Etta's, and carried on regardless.

"Many consider my brother to be a suspect and dismiss his statement as lies, but we're not the kind of people to lay the blame on an innocent, as they've done with him. We're not made of *that* stuff."

"That's very noble of you, and I hope the authorities will soon be just as convinced of Mr Petronio's innocence..."

"In fact, they already are. You see, my brother wasn't kept in custody yesterday after the carabinieri interviewed him. It's normal in murder cases to suspect close family and friends first, but my brother was cleared beyond any possible doubts."

"Was he?" Etta tried desperately to conceal her disappointment.

"I wasn't here, Mrs Passolina," he said, taking over from his sister. "The day my wife passed away, I was in Rome on business. I was to come back yesterday evening, but when the carabinieri called me, I dropped everything and came back to Castelmezzano as soon as I could."

"Were you staying with your sister and brother-in-law?" Etta asked, wondering whether or not it was an appropriate question.

"No, I was participating in a seminar in Villa Mantegna, situated in the southern part of Rome. Agrippina and Domizio live too far from there, and as it was only for two nights, I decided to use the conference hotel."

"When he called us yesterday morning," Agrippina explained, "my brother was so shocked that I decided to accompany him home. Domizio had an important meeting and could not come with us, but I drove over to Claudio's hotel to fetch him, and then we hurried back to Castelmezzano."

ADRIANA LICIO

"And you left your own car at the hotel?" Etta asked the man without giving either of them time to think.

He looked at her with a twinkle in his eyes, despite his sorrow. "I left my car at Potenza train station. I never drive to Rome; I prefer the train."

Etta flushed; Claudio had guessed the reason behind her question. Nonetheless, she made a quick mental calculation: if he was in Rome without a car, there was no way he could have come back to Castelmezzano and returned to his hotel overnight. There was no public transport at night, and even if he'd rented a car, it still would have taken over four hours to get to Castelmezzano and back to Rome. The carabinieri must have checked his statements and train tickets, and surely they'd checked the GPS on his mobile phone too. That's why they hadn't kept him in custody. The man had a solid alibi.

"And now that I have cleared my name, madam, do you want to tell me about your house?"

And Etta launched herself into a long and painful description of her financial position, the meagre pension, the affection she had for the dear place, but how impossible it would be for her to keep it in the future.

"Rationality is such an important factor when you're doing business," he said approvingly. "Selling now can only save you money in the long term. And this is the right moment to sell – we have a foreign investor looking for high-quality accommodation to turn into a profitable luxury B&B."

Etta could not help a deep sigh.

"I understand it must be painful," he smiled at her, but Etta was sure she had spotted a greedy light illuminating his black eyes, "but as you said, maintenance is rather expensive nowadays, especially on larger properties. If a profitable business is taking care of the building, you'll never have to see it go to rack and ruin. I'm glad you chose my agency as I'm certain we can strike a good deal for you."

"Do I need to sign a contract?"

"Yes, a mandate for the agency to sell, to guarantee our exclusivity. But first I should come to visit your house for a full evaluation."

"And I'd also need to buy or rent a small flat."

"Again, you're in luck. I own a splendid modern apartment building in Pietrapertosa, and can offer you a large and airy two-room apartment at a nominal rent," and he named the very property Dora lived in. "Go and think over the whole thing in the peace and quiet of your own home, but please – and I speak as a friend – don't waste your time. Let's not lose this opportunity. I'll call my client straight away and tell them we have a potential A-class property – I wouldn't like them to buy something else now that I've spoken to you."

Agrippina accompanied Etta to the door, thanking her for the visit.

"I've seen my brother reacting to the whole thing positively for the first time," she gripped Etta's arm with a firm hand. "Thanks so much for coming."

Etta made an effort not to cry "Ouch!" Instead, she fired off another question.

"Why didn't you go to stay in Villa Chiara?" she asked, stopping on the threshold. "I imagine you'd have more peace and quiet there than here, and not as many memories."

"That's true, it would be better for my brother to be away from this house for a while. But Villa Chiara has been closed for so long – unfortunately, I don't manage to come down here as often as I'd like. But you're right, if Domizio gets a chance to join us, he can do some gardening and late spring cleaning to spruce up the house so we can all move in there for a while..."

"I'm only mentioning it," Etta added, all innocence, "because I heard you were the victims of a nasty attack yesterday when you came out of the carabinieri station."

A flash of hatred distorted Agrippina's face.

"News travels fast in these villages. That's all too true. Miss

Sventura is a rather sly creature, so let's just say that attack is often one's best defence."

And with that, Agrippina wished her farewell and closed the door. Etta was out in the street, it was almost midday and the sun was shining and warm, but she felt a sudden cold freeze both her heart and body.

Miss Sventura, Agrippina had said. Yes, of course, the witch's name was Cassandra Sventura. How hadn't she realised that before? CS were the initials on the shard of the terracotta jar. Had Cassandra had been there with Sibilla that night? Were they celebrating some witchcraft rites? Etta stopped in horror as more thoughts swirled around her head. Had something gone wrong? Or had hatred sprung up between the two witches? And she had sent Dora straight into the wolf's lair.

With trembling hands, she took her mobile phone from her bag, but Dora's number was not reachable. Putting it hastily back, she hurried along the Path of the Seven Stones, regretting that she wasn't half as fit as she wished to be.

8

THE WITCH'S HOME

Dora climbed up through the narrow alleys and steps that made up the Rabatana, the old Arabian quarter of Pietrapertosa. There were no longer many people living there; in the labyrinth of passages, you couldn't reach your home with either a car or a shopping trolley. And nowadays, people didn't use mules to transport their goods. But a few brave souls of all ages felt they couldn't live anywhere else.

In a little white stuccoed building, hidden in a passageway mostly made up of the backs of other houses, lay Cassandra Sventura's home. Dora used the brass knocker to announce her presence and a woman with long dark hair and glaring carbon eyes opened the door, leaving it ajar.

"What do you want?"

"Hello, dear, I baked some of my biscuits for you. I knew you were a good friend of poor Sibilla and I thought you might need some company."

That morning, Cassandra had shut her door in the face of many a villager, but Dorotea Rosa Pepe had been the only woman to visit her with food in the past when she had fallen sick. Though she had never been one of Cassandra's clients, Dora had always treated her as a neighbour and an important part of the community. Also, the old teacher would greet her, even in crowded places when other villagers pretended not to see her.

After a moment of hesitation, Cassandra opened the door.

"Come in, Miss Pepe."

Dora entered a light and airy living room with a tiny balcony suspended over the village rocks. She remembered how surprised she'd been the first time she'd visited; she had expected to enter a dark grotto with mysterious signs and little or no light, but Cassandra's home was as normal as any other house. Almost. Only if you were very observant would you notice that the landscape paintings on the wall featured magic places scattered around the country: an ancient oak tree; a mysterious well; a congregation of witches; a modern painting of cabalistic signs and symbols.

Two black cats with green eyes shining like lanterns in the night came forward, pretending indifference, to smell the newcomer. Dora bent to caress the one closer to her.

"Watch out!" Cassandra warned, but the cat was enjoying the caresses around her ears, purring with pleasure.

"Tenebra seems to like you. She's not usually too nice to people she doesn't know."

"This is the kitten you rescued last year, isn't she?"

"Some boys were really awful to the poor little one, no wonder she doesn't trust people. Well, most people. But please, take a seat."

Dora chose a comfy armchair next to a cabinet filled with labelled jars and dark bottles.

"You were friends with Sibilla, weren't you?"

Cassandra emitted a long, deep sigh. "We were more than friends, we were sisters."

"You mean in your Art?" Dora, as did most villagers, knew both the official and unofficial genealogy of every fellow citizen. She was in no doubt that the two women could not have been real sisters.

"That's a bond stronger than blood," said Cassandra, reading her thoughts. "When he killed her, a part of me died with her."

Dora tried to take hold of her hand to comfort her, but Cassandra retracted like a wild animal not used to tenderness of any sort. Even Tenebra the cat was tamer than she.

"I heard you shouting at Claudio last night..."

"Where were you? Are you a witch yourself?" Cassandra asked, her black eyes widening in surprise, her whole body tensing as if ready to attack.

"I was close to the convent. None of you noticed me, but I witnessed the whole scene."

Cassandra's nostrils moved as if she were a weasel in search of a scent, as if she could smell lies. She found no traces and relaxed just a tiny bit.

"I see," she said.

"Do you really believe he murdered his wife?"

Cassandra took a long pause before answering. "No. The strange thing is that I don't *feel* he killed her, but I *think* he did. The Art doesn't always let me see things in detail; at times, I only get a few glimpses, other times a complete vision. This time I just felt the claws..."

"The claws?"

"It was the full moon, so I had gone to the Witches' Cave. Sibilla had sent me a message – she wasn't going to come. I did my dance in the night; it was beautiful. I saw her and she saw me. We were happy. Even separated, we could do things together, and our powers grew stronger."

"And then?"

"I went back home. I did all the rites, for sleeping doesn't come easily after a Sabbath. Lying in bed, I was already in the world of dreams when I felt two claws around my neck. I couldn't breathe, I couldn't scream. I saw Sibilla and felt all her pain. Then I woke up and knew she was no more."

Dora brought her hands up to her mouth, as if she had been present to witness the scene.

"But you don't actually know if it was he who killed her?"

"The Art decided not to show me, but who else could it be? I'm also a human and I know of human things. Sibilla had told me about her husband's debts. He was after her money."

"But the carabinieri set him free last night..."

"I need not the material proof they're after to know the truth."

"Most people think exactly like you," said Dora softly, "that he's guilty, so maybe it's just a matter of time before the carabinieri find the evidence."

"Human justice can be very slow, and it can take the wrong path," Cassandra said as a quiet despair crossed her face, which had been so animated up to that point.

"But if you were at the Witches' Cave, that explains the findings..."

"What findings?" Cassandra asked, looking straight into her eyes.

"There was the shard of a terracotta jar," blabbered Dora, "with two letters on it, C and S. Only when I was at your door did I remember they're your initials."

Cassandra looked shocked, but she was clearly trying her best not to show it. She muttered something like "That can't be", then came back to her senses.

"Can I offer you a cup of tea?"

"That'd be lovely, we can try my biscuits too."

Cassandra disappeared into the kitchen and was gone for a good five minutes. When she returned to Dora, she was holding a small tray, a cup containing a dark steamy liquid and a honey jar on top of it.

"I think I'll have it without honey," said Dora, taking the hot cup with both her hands.

"Oh no, it has a rather strong taste. You'd be better adding at least one spoonful, maybe two."

Dora did as she was told and stirred the liquid. It wasn't black as it had at first seemed, but rather a deep, dark red.

"Aren't you taking any?" Dora asked.

"No, I had a cup just before you arrived."

Cassandra's piercing eyes were on her again, not leaving her face, her eyes, her hand on the spoon. Dora quietly lifted the cup to her lips. The liquid tasted bitter despite the honey and she couldn't hide a grimace of disgust. But Cassandra was still watching closely, her lips twitching as if whispering some magic formula.

Under the spell of those hypnotic eyes, Dora lifted the cup to her lips for a second gulp. As the steamy liquid infused her mouth, her throat, her chest, the shouts came from outside.

"Dora? Dora? Are you OK, Dora?"

Then there was a heavy pounding on the front door.

"Carabinieri here," a male voice shouted. "Open the door."

Cassandra shivered, a flash of anguish in her eyes, then she took back control and opened the door. The brigadiere entered with two other men. The cats arched their backs and hissed like wild beasts ready to attack, but Cassandra whispered something soft to them that didn't sound like a human language at all and the felines calmed, still scrutinising the newcomers.

"You're under arrest for the murder of Sibilla Petronio. You have the right to remain silent…" The brigadiere completed the formalities with some trepidation as the other two carabinieri put handcuffs on the woman's wrists.

Screaming and protesting rose from outside.

"I've told you once, let me in. Now!"

Etta squirmed in between the black uniformed carabinieri and landed in the living room. She saw Dora still sitting on the armchair, her face stunned and a cup in her hands.

"Oh, Dora dear, are you OK?"

"I most certainly am. What's happening?"

"I'll tell you soon. Let's leave this place."

Etta took her cup away and led her friend out of the house. But as they passed Cassandra, the woman whispered to Dora.

"Now you can see. Use the gift."

Before she could add any more, the carabinieri dragged the witch towards their car, parked on the outskirts of the Rabatana in the upper part of the village. Etta wanted to hurry Dora down the tiny street and on towards her block of flats, but Dora stopped her.

"Let me see to the cats." She walked back up the alley and pushed open the lower part of the door to make sure the animals could come and go at their leisure. She'd be back later to feed them and put the recycling bin outside for collection, if the carabinieri really meant to keep Cassandra in custody.

"Did you drink that tea?" Etta asked.

"A few gulps."

"Oh my goodness, are you OK?"

"Of course I am."

"You don't think it was poisoned, do you?"

"Poisoned? Why should it be?"

"Maybe Cassandra wanted to do you in."

Dora burst into a gentle laugh. "Surely not. Why did they arrest her?"

"I've got quite a few things to tell you, but let's go to your flat. Here in the Rabatana, there are too many darkened windows and hidden eyes spying on us…"

9

THE SEEDLING OF AN IDEA

When they reached Dora's flat, Etta was shocked to see how ugly the building was. Inside, Dora had created a nice environment full of plants cascading down from cupboards and shelves, and a splendid Ficus Benjamina occupied a good part of the rather small living room, but despite the sunny day, the flat was gloomy. It not only faced north, but the one small window was overlooked by another building that was far too close.

And this is where Claudio wants to house me, thought Etta.

Etta told Dora all that had happened at the Petronios' house, and Dora told Etta about her conversation with Cassandra.

"Are you sure you're OK?" asked Etta once more, unable to let go of the image of the tea cup.

"Of course, I'm fine."

"Maybe we should go to the hospital for a check-up."

"A check-up for what?"

"Don't you see? You told Cassandra you'd found a shard of her jar, with her initials printed on it, at the crime scene. Maybe she wanted to get rid of you so you couldn't tell anyone else and served you some poison."

"Nonsense, I'm fine, and alive."

"Maybe it's a slow acting poison…"

"You're scaring me. And anyway, I trust Cassandra implicitly. We should help her out."

"Dora, you're over sixty. You should have learned not to trust people by now."

"What reason would she have had to kill Sibilla?"

"Well, you know how women can be with other women," Etta said, displaying an uncharacteristic patience as she explained a few things to Dora about human nature. "Sibilla was a beauty, and Cassandra is not. Maybe she was insanely jealous of her. Maybe Cassandra is in love with Claudio. Maybe the two witches had a quarrel over some potion, or Sibilla claimed to be a more powerful witch and Cassandra is a psychopath. Wickedness can walk many paths."

"Not one of the things you mentioned convinces me."

Etta was flabbergasted. She'd thought Dora was a sweet, harmless thing she could manipulate at will. Where had this stubborn mule with all her certainties come from all of a sudden?

"But someone must have killed her," Etta said finally in her best ice-cold teacher's voice. "I don't think Sibilla managed to strangle herself with her own hands. As for the husband, he certainly was the main suspect, but he has an irrefutable alibi. You even mentioned that your beloved Cassandra doesn't *feel* he's the killer. Who else would have an interest in doing her in?"

"That I don't know, but certainly not Cassandra."

"She's definitely bewitched you if she didn't poison you."

To make sure Dora didn't start convulsing and die of poisoning in the hours that followed, Etta decided to stay with her for lunch, despite the feeling of claustrophobia the dismal flat gave her. Dora, in the meantime, had taken out her pasta board, large enough to occupy at least half of the galley-style kitchen, and quickly prepared some delicious orecchiette. Her hands moving fast on the board, she rolled the dough into a long, thin snake. She then cut it into pieces and stretched the small cubes of pasta using a knife, shaping them over her thumb with a few precise movements. Minutes later, as the pasta boiled, she deep fried rapini with garlic, anchovies and chilli in olive oil. It was as delicious a lunch as Etta had once a month when she headed to a restaurant with her book club friends.

Funnily enough, they didn't speak of the murder anymore, but instead dedicated their conversation to the charm of travel and the list of places they really wanted to see. It was as if their meagre pensions were actually gold mines and they could pack their bags and go at a moment's notice.

"You know what, Etta dear?" said Dora all of a sudden, her slate-grey eyes shining with enthusiasm.

"What?"

"Those low cost companies – we could scan their offers, do our best to save up enough money, and maybe once or twice a year, we could manage a long weekend somewhere."

"Forget it." Etta waved the idea away impatiently.

"Why not? At times, flight tickets can be as cheap as a coach fare to Naples."

"Then they add a tenner for every item you take – a tenner for your purse, another for your bag, another to get to the front of the queue, taxes, even the oxygen you'll breathe during the flight."

Dora gave a laugh. "I'll be extra careful to read all the small print."

Etta was squirming in her seat and twisting her hands, for once seeming strangely embarrassed.

"You won't tell anybody, will you?"

"Of course not, but I don't know what I'm not supposed to tell them," said Dora.

"I'm… I'm… I'm against people flying."

"You're *what*?"

Etta sighed, half angry, half sad. "I can't fly. I'm simply terrified at the idea."

"Oh," said Dora, and Etta could see the huge disappointment pulling every single feature of her round face downwards. The corners of her lips, the curve of her eyes, even her chubby cheeks seemed to deflate and sag. "I see." Dora thought it over before adding, without much conviction, "There are international coaches..."

"Sure, three days to reach London, where we'd have to spend another three days with our feet up to recover from swollen legs. Coaches are only for the younger generations."

"You're right, I never fancied coaches. I'd love to travel by train, but they're awfully expensive."

Etta nodded, feeling guilty at being the weak party on this occasion.

THEY CONTINUED TO CHAT UNTIL THE BELLS OUTSIDE CHIMED FIVE o'clock, and a phone call reminded them that the carabinieri were waiting for them at the station to take their fingerprints.

"As if we're a couple of criminals," Etta growled at the small, shy carabiniere who had been tasked with the terrifying duty. But despite the scary woman's best attempts to get him talking, he didn't say a word about the case. Within 15 minutes, the two women were outside again and Etta decided it was time to go home. The seedling of an idea was germinating in her mind, a crazy notion that she needed to think about before sharing it with Dora.

Dora accompanied her to where the mule track started, and Etta turned to her with a question.

"Dora, do you own a car?"

"Yes, a yellow Fiat 500. Don't you remember it?"

Of course she did. Wasn't it Dora's first car – the one her parents had given her as a gift when she passed her driving test? Yes, it was that very car. Dora had never changed it.

"Does it still work?"

"It's a marvel, the mechanic says they no longer build cars

like that. But," she sighed deeply, "I might have to sell it. Insurance, taxes – just more costs."

"I'd better go. I had come to cheer you up, but now we're just getting depressed. Are you sure you're completely OK? No gurgling stomach? Dizziness? Any of that stuff?"

"I'm absolutely fine," replied Dora firmly. "I'm going to see that Cassandra's cats get their food."

They walked together for a short while, then Etta was on her own on the Path of the Seven Stones, finally free to think. And the strange thing was that Etta was thinking of Dora more than herself.

"The poor woman, living in such an awful place. So dark, with its low, oppressive ceilings and no decent windows. It's a trap rather than a home. We have two homes between us, one of them too large, and two cars. Certainly there'd be other benefits. On the other hand, it won't be easy..."

And actually, she felt so uneasy and uncertain that by the time she got home, she had an uncharacteristic urge to call her daughter in Granada.

"Hi, Mum, how are you?"

"Fine, fine."

"I've just heard about poor Sibilla's accident yesterday. Wasn't she the local witch?"

"Yes, she was."

"I'm so sorry, I wonder who will learn the Art now that she's no longer..."

Etta thought better than to tell Maddalena anything she knew, especially that it had been she who'd found the body. She certainly wasn't going to be mentioning that it wasn't an accident, but murder.

"I've called you to ask your opinion on something. Do you remember Miss Dorotea Rosa Pepe?"

"Your colleague in Pietrapertosa? Of course I do."

"What would you think if I were to share my house with her?

We'd divide the expenses, run one car and keep each other company."

"I'd say it's a great idea," Maddalena said in a thoughtful, icy tone devoid of enthusiasm. "Except, Mum, you'd dominate the poor woman. She'd become your slave and have no way out."

"What are you saying?"

"Mum, honestly, you should be aware of what you're like by now. You'd torment her and make her life miserable. It would be your rules, and I really can't imagine *anyone* sharing their life with you. You remember…"

"Stop there, I understand," and Etta put down the phone.

Bugger off, Maddalena. Children always look at their parents as tyrants. It would be enough to set up a contract, agreeing on some basic rules. Yes, she'd write a contract, ask Dora her opinion and see what she said. That way, the poor woman could leave that ugly place she was living in now, Etta could keep her beloved house, they'd sell one car, and maybe even have enough money left for a little trip every now and then. Perhaps train companies did special offers for elderly people, provided they booked a couple of years in advance and managed to live long enough to take the trip. She'd write her side of the contract first, and then speak to Dora, ask her to read it and feel free to add more clauses herself. A clear contract was the reasonable way to resolve most differences of opinion. Now, wasn't that a splendid idea?

Etta took a piece of paper and started to jot down a few ideas. What were the likely points of conflict? In theory, the use of the kitchen, but from what she had seen over the past couple of days, it'd be better to leave the cooking part to Dora. Etta would do the dishes and the cleaning – not very creative, but hadn't work specialisation saved the human race?

Bathroom. The one upstairs was very small, so they'd have to agree on times to use the larger one downstairs. After all, it would only be the two of them.

Pets. That was an essential point. She knew Dora had had a

cat before it passed away, but on this she had to be firm. No pets would ever be allowed under the same roof as her as long as she lived. Actually, afterwards as well. She would haunt anyone who brought a furry, peeing thing into her house, even generations after she'd passed away.

Car. Well, Dora was going to sell her useless Fiat 500 anyway. And as they became older, they'd need a more comfy car. Etta's estate car would undoubtedly do better.

Bedroom – no problems there. Dora could inspect the guest room and decide if she preferred that or Maddalena's former bedroom. They were both larger than her entire flat.

Guests. That might become a contentious issue. At times, Maddalena and her dumb hubby would come to visit, but that only happened once or twice a year, so Dora would have to put up with it. But would Dora have guests of her own? Maybe that stupid nephew of hers, Arturo. And she, Etta, would have to put up with that. The important thing was to agree on some reasonable limits.

Men. Could there still be men in their lives? Surely not, but just to be clear, she'd better insert a clause. If either party invited a man home… then what? If Dora decided to get married, she was free to do so of course, and it'd be Etta's problem to deal with the high running costs of her own house. But what if she, Etta, met a man? Would she throw her friend out? Etta was selfish, but not totally unfair.

She sighed, unable to reach a satisfactory conclusion. Men always seemed to be trouble, even when they were hypothetical. She left that line of the contract blank. Maybe Dora would come up with a better idea.

General cleaning once a week for each woman. And they'd draw up an exact list of what 'cleaning' meant.

Rubbish. Who would take the rubbish out? They'd take it in turns.

Etta felt her eyelids getting heavier and heavier, and she slid into her bed. The murderer had been caught, she had found a way to keep her dear house, the world looked a better place and she could have nice dreams. She saw in her mind's eye the explosion of yellow brooms on the Path of the Seven Stones, then Villa Chiara's pretty roses, her enjoyment of them spoiled by the rubbish collection. But who else had mentioned rubbish? Oh yes, Dora was going to put out the recycling bin at Cassandra's. And putting out the rubbish was the last item Etta had written on the contract. But it wasn't just that – there was something wrong about the rubbish. Was she dreaming? No, there was definitely something niggling her to do with the rubbish.

Her hand crawled from her pillow to the bedside table until she found the switch and turned on the lamp. What was it? Oh yes, the rubbish. Why think of that now? Was it the power of dreams and night-time imagery, or had she really been forming a strong theory in her mind? What were its implications?

She gasped in horror, her mind finally clearing like a strong gust of wind had blown the clouds from Castelmezzano. She could see for miles. Could the truth be that perverse, that well thought out? Was that why he had an alibi? And what about her – was her husband involved too? He had to be.

And Dora – Dora had never doubted it was tea, not poison in her cup.

Etta got out of bed and walked in circles, her mind working frantically as it ran through the sequence of events and tested her theory. When the first glimmer of daylight shone behind the shutters, she was slouching in her armchair, exhausted not from lack of sleep, but from waiting.

As soon as she was sure he would have arrived at the carabinieri station, she made her phone call and asked to speak to Maresciallo Gaggio. He listened, he expressed his disbelief, he said he'd call her back. And one long hour later, the phone rang and he said nothing had been in the paper bin, and the most he could find was ash in the fireplace. Hard to claim that as evidence. They argued, they debated fiercely, then they came to an arrangement.

Etta sat back, discomfited at the idea of more waiting. Everything had turned upside down. What about all her glorious plans for the house that she had made only a few hours earlier? Well, it now looked like she would have to get Claudio Petronio round to value it after all.

10

THE POWER OF HABITS

It was six o'clock in the evening when Etta's doorbell rang, and she opened her door to find Claudio and Agrippina's obsequious faces smiling at her.

"I'm very glad you made up your mind, Mrs Passolina," Claudio said, clumsily holding her hand for longer than necessary. "That's the right decision. I can see from the outside how large this house is. Far too expensive for a retired teacher."

"I feel so…" Etta sighed, allowing them in and retracting her hand. "But I can't tell you how much I appreciate the two of you being here. Before taking the final decision, though, I'd love to have an idea of how much the house is worth."

"My brother insisted we come as soon as possible, for your sake," Agrippina said, sliding keenly into the house and looking around. Room by room, Etta showed them everything. She could see Agrippina's eyes glittering with greed, but Claudio's head kept shaking sadly in disapproval.

"This is so badly organised, Mrs Passolina. I mean, no offence, of course, it's not your fault. It's something we see all the time: old houses were organised in a completely different way to modern standards; a way that's now considered hopelessly old fashioned."

Agrippina kept silent, but her eyes were either on her brother, as if to prompt him on what to say next, or on Etta to catch every single particular.

"Do you think so?" Etta exclaimed in disbelief.

"See this bathroom?" he said as they looked around upstairs. "Three bedrooms and one small bathroom. As I told you, our investor is interested in turning your property into a B&B, and it'd be inappropriate…"

A shiver went down Etta's spine. A B&B in her house? Even though she managed to contain her disappointment, she found it hard to say what she had to say next.

"Well, with the bedrooms being so large, it wouldn't be difficult to fit en suite bathrooms as needed."

Brother and sister burst into condescending laughter.

"Mrs Passolina, really," Claudio said, as incredulously as if she had suggested they could create an Olympic swimming pool on her terrace. "If you had my experience, you'd know how hard it is to do any kind of construction work in an old house. This building most likely dates from the early XIX century; they didn't have the benefit of reinforced concrete in those times. Whenever you so much as touch a wall, you don't know what effect it's going to have on the whole structure."

"So you're saying they won't be able to fit en suites?"

"Of course they will," he said patiently, "but it will cost more than they'll pay to buy the house in the first place."

"Oh, come on!" Etta cried.

"Mrs Passolina," said Agrippina, sounding offended. She'd hardly intervened, but her role in leading the whole conversation was still obvious. "May I remind you that my brother has been in this job for decades?"

"I'm afraid old houses are just a source of trouble," Claudio added in a soothing voice.

They finished their inspection and Etta invited them to sit on the sofa as she prepared a cup of coffee. She came back with her best silver tray and porcelain cups. Again, she felt sure she spotted a greedy gleam in both brother and sister's eyes as they looked at the shining tray.

"As you'll be moving into a much smaller place," Agrippina said, "you might consider selling the house as it is, with all its furniture and antique pieces in place."

Etta was startled. "Really? I was thinking of taking most of them into my new home. These pieces have been in my family for generations."

"I don't think they'll fit in," Agrippina said dryly.

"You see, modern flats have low ceilings," Claudio's voice was supercilious, as if he felt he had to educate this obstinate client of his, "so you won't have to spend a fortune on heating," and he pointed to the old ebony library shelves, taking up a whole wall from floor to ceiling, then to the tall cupboard on the other side of the room.

"But won't it be very hot in summer?"

"Not at all," he reassured her. "The flats I rent out face north, so they can be fresh and pleasant in summer too."

"Seems to me they're mostly facing the big building in front of them."

"That shields them from the wind."

With trembling lips, Etta found the courage to ask the most important question.

"Well, now you've seen the house, I guess you're able to say – how much do you think it's worth?"

Claudio got his jotter out of his bag, ran some multiplications on a small calculator housed in the leather folder of his notepad, glanced around as if to catch some final details.

"I'd say the value of this property is around €25,000, but…"

He was cut short by Etta's scream. "€25,000?"

"But," he gave her a scornful look, "I believe my investor might understand your position and appreciate your house, so I suggest we ask for €30,000."

"Are you kidding me?"

"Madam!"

"I mean, this is a noble old house..."

"It's certainly old," Agrippina sneered.

"It has a large terrace, which is a rarity in Castelmezzano."

"Ah yes, the terrace," Agrippina said disparagingly, looking up at her brother as if deferring to a learned professor.

"Terraces," Claudio said, caressing his moustache, "are valued at one third of the square metre price of the house."

"But the view..."

"No one pays for a view, Mrs Passolina," said Agrippina bluntly.

Claudio nodded. "That's correct. Views have no market price."

"And the high ceilings, the large rooms..."

"They only mean higher running costs, as you well know, otherwise you would not be thinking of selling. Big houses were fashionable in the past when families had servants and labour was cheap. Now, this house needs decorating inside and out, and I can tell you that outside painting will cost a fortune."

Etta nodded. That much she knew. "Nonetheless," she added, this time with a lack of conviction, "I thought the house value would be at least ten times this much."

Agrippina and Claudio burst into loud laughter.

"I'm sorry," he said, finally recovering. "You're not in Potenza. Villages are being abandoned as young people move to towns and cities, and the house market in Castelmezzano is plummeting. I don't want to rush you into things, madam, but I wouldn't waste time either. The investor is here, but he will soon find something else, and believe me, I have plenty of pretty houses that have been sitting unsold for years. Nobody wants them. No one buys houses in remote villages."

"Why should they?" Agrippina asked. "They'd have to drive 30km just to fuel their cars. No trains, 30 minutes to reach the highway and almost 50 minutes to get to Potenza. That's clearly not what modern folk look for."

"It's a difficult time for the property market in the whole

country," added Claudio. "But in small villages, it's stagnation. Property values are depreciating rapidly."

"Trust my brother," whispered Agrippina, hardly able to contain her triumphant smile. "He has your best interests at heart. He's been in this trade forever, so he wants only the best for his clients."

"But it's so hard for me to let go." Etta finally collapsed, her eyes watery despite all her efforts not to crumble.

"We all like to hang on to our familiar habits," Agrippina said, sitting beside Etta on her sofa as if to console her, "but you'll see – you'll soon get used to your new flat. It will be so easy to maintain. You'll do your cleaning in a bat of the eyelashes."

Etta raised her gaze to Agrippina and locked eyes with her.

"I'm glad you mentioned the word 'habits'. Isn't it strange how we stick to them, even when we shouldn't?"

Agrippina tilted her head, as if she thought grief over losing the house had sent Etta's brain out of kilter.

"Frankly, I don't know what on earth you're talking about, Mrs Passolina."

"I should explain myself better," apologised Etta, uncharacteristically meekly. "We're so used to doing certain things – let's say putting the rubbish out for collection – that we do them even when we're not supposed to. For example, when we want to lead people to believe a house has been empty for quite some time."

"I don't see what your point is…" but Agrippina's face had become livid, her lips tightening in an expressionless grin.

"Silly me, I'm so bad at explaining myself," Etta continued, pressing her cheeks between her palms as if she were a fragile old lady. "You see, on the morning I found your sister-in-law's body, Miss Pepe and I walked back to Castelmezzano and saw the municipal waste truck collecting the rubbish from Villa Chiara. But you said you hadn't been there for weeks, or even months."

"What does it matter?" Agrippina asked, shaking her head, her back straight, her head up.

"It matters because while Claudio was in Rome, establishing the perfect alibi, his beloved sister and brother-in-law were in Castelmezzano, inviting Sibilla to Villa Chiara where they strangled her, leaving her body at the Witches' Cave once Cassandra had finished her rites and setting the scene for them to get away with murder."

"That's absurd! You must be out of your mind. My sister-in-law's murderer has been arrested and is already in jail."

"Yes, your plan to frame Cassandra seems to have worked – for now. You watched while she hid her jar in the cave, then took it out and broke it, and made sure to leave the fragment with her initials on it in full view."

"Claudio, tell this woman she's nothing but a lunatic."

"You're mad, Mrs Passolina," Claudio said, despite the horror painted on his face. "What a pity you don't have a single shred of evidence..."

"Yes, that would be a pity," Etta cut him short, "except that Cassandra never got rid of the message she received from Sibilla, saying she couldn't be at the Sabbath because that night, she was meant to visit you and your husband, Agrippina."

And Etta waved a letter written in spiky, almost illegible script in front of their noses.

"It was stupid of you, if you will allow me to say that, to go to all the trouble of destroying Cassandra's jar, but not check her house to see whether or not she still had Sibilla's message."

"A written note?" Agrippina cried.

"Yes," Etta nodded triumphantly, "you should have known witches communicate in the old way. She asked Marcellino, the butcher's boy, to take her note to Cassandra in Pietrapertosa."

"Didn't Sibilla say she just phoned her?" Claudio asked his sister fiercely.

"That's what she told me," Agrippina replied, swallowing.

"Then what's that paper the old biddy's holding?" roared Claudio. "I told you it was a stupid plan."

"Oh, shut up, you useless good-for-nothing. The only way to save your stupid skin from all the trouble you've got yourself into was to get rid of Sibilla. You should be thanking me, and my husband, for killing your wife and setting that witch up to take the blame, while you swanned around in Rome, establishing your alibi so no one would suspect you."

"I didn't ask..."

"Let me speak to this woman." Agrippina cut him short, then addressed Etta with a mellow voice and a sinister smile. "I'm sure you haven't told anybody yet, have you?"

"That's true, but I'm going to the carabinieri right now..."

"No, you won't." Agrippina jumped up. With her hands around Etta's neck, she cried to her brother, "Come and help me, she's strong."

Etta kicked out and fought fiercely with her arms, but when Claudio joined his sister, she let out a cry.

"Help, HELLLP! What the heck are you waiting...?"

The two cruel hands were now four and all seemed to go foggy as her lungs and whole body cried out for oxygen.

"Halt! Let go of Mrs Passolina," Maresciallo Gaggio cried, emerging from the storeroom beneath the stairs. From behind the terrace shutter, Brigadiere Marazzi appeared, his gun pointing towards the brother and sister. Too shocked to argue, they let Etta go.

"In the name of the Italian law, we declare you under arrest..." The brigadiere went through the formalities as more carabinieri surged into the house and handcuffed Claudio and Agrippina.

"And many thanks," the maresciallo announced when the brigadiere had finished, "for your frank and honest confession, and attempt to kill one more person so we could catch you red-handed."

As the carabinieri accompanied the protesting siblings

outside, Etta collapsed on the sofa, groaning and massaging her neck.

"Were you waiting to increase the victim count?" she growled at Gaggio.

"That will give them an even harsher sentence," said the maresciallo, smiling.

Etta gave him a dirty look.

"We just wanted to make sure their course of action was clear in the video we took." As he turned towards a small camera set up on top of Etta's TV, Dora came in through the door to hug her friend and ask if she was OK.

"I'm OK, though I've got far too clear an idea of what poor Sibilla went through. Suffocation is an awful way to die."

"But how did you guess it was the three of them?"

"Yes, exactly," acknowledged Gaggio. "Once we cleared Claudio Petronio, we didn't think to check his sister and her husband."

"They had organised what they believed to be the perfect murder. With Claudio being able to prove he was elsewhere and therefore beyond suspicion, no one would think his sister had acted as the hitman. If only she hadn't decided to come back to Castelmezzano with her brother and mention that Villa Chiara had been closed up for weeks, maybe I would never have thought twice about the rubbish being collected that morning."

"But she was a control freak," the maresciallo said, nodding. "Overnight, she and her husband returned to Rome, soon after killing Sibilla and framing Cassandra. Agrippina could have stayed in Rome, but she wanted to ensure her brother didn't make any mistakes, so she came back with him under the guise of concerned sister."

"How did you know Agrippina's husband was involved too?" asked Dora.

"Ah, that was a lucky guess," said Etta. "You've seen how thin Agrippina is – it's unlikely she would have the strength to carry a dead body all the way to the Witches' Cave by herself. I believe Agrippina went on ahead to spy on Cassandra, find out exactly where she hid her jar, then alerted Domizio by text when the witch had finished her Sabbath rites, and he brought the body up to the spot."

"That's a lot of work for him…"

"Have you seen the man?" said Etta scornfully. "He may be big and strong and muscly, but he's really a little mouse who'd jump off a cliff if his wife asked him to. He'd do anything for her without question."

"But how are you going to prove he was here too?"

"It will be enough to track their mobile phone movements," replied the maresciallo.

"But what about Claudio, will he end up in jail?" wondered Etta. "After all, he wasn't directly involved in the murder."

"But he planned the whole thing with his sister. He's the mastermind and I'm sure the judge will take that into account."

"What about poor Cassandra?" asked Dora, her hands over her heart.

"She will be immediately set free with all our apologies, Miss Pepe."

Etta slid her bum closer to Dora's on the sofa and hugged her friend, saying, "It was your stubborn conviction that Cassandra was innocent that set my brain going."

"What I don't understand," Dora said, relieved to know that Cassandra would soon be back home with her cats, "is why you didn't arrest Agrippina the moment Etta found the letter in which Sibilla said she was visiting her and her husband in Villa Chiara?"

Etta handed her the letter she was still holding and Dora read through it without understanding.

"But that's your handwriting!"

"Exactly, but Agrippina doesn't know that, and Claudio, like most men, hardly takes any notice of what's right in front of him. And I have to say, my handwriting is very similar to poor Sibilla's…"

Dora gazed at her friend without understanding.

"When I was at Claudio's home, I saw Sibilla's handwriting, all spiky and thorny and illegible, just like mine…"

"Apart from the waste collection at Villa Chiara," Maresciallo Gaggio explained, "which was scant evidence indeed, we had no real proof. That's why we had to set this scene up and hope it would result in a confession, or even a new crime. We were lucky and got both."

EPILOGUE

"You'd better be careful, you don't want to damage my house," cried Etta, angry at the carelessness of the two removals men. They sighed. It was hard work with the fearsome Mrs Concetta Natale Passolina scrutinising their every move. Luckily, they had just carried in the last piece of furniture that Dora had taken from her dingy flat to join her in her new room at Etta's.

As the men left with a grin of satisfaction, Dora clasped her hands together and said, "I can't believe I'm out of that prison", looking with delight at her new living room. A huge number of plants were already on the terrace, waiting to be transplanted into shiny new terracotta urns. Dora had given up her dream to have a pet, but only on the condition that a whole forest of plants would be allowed to grow inside and outside her new home. Etta had given in quite easily; she didn't mind having plants all around. Actually, she loved the idea, especially as they'd be luscious and thriving when tended by Dora's loving hand. What she couldn't stand were the withered, dying plants she used to have.

But it was Dora's other changes in the contract that had surprised her. Sweet, reasonable Dora would not give up her car by any means, and in the end, out of sheer desperation, Etta had sold her car and agreed they'd stick with the uncomfortable Fiat 500. Once they had decided on duties and spaces and guests, though, Etta had rejoiced at the idea she would no longer need to sell her house. By sharing expenses, they could even manage to save a little for travelling. And that's exactly where Etta, to her own amazement, had agreed with Dora that they'd subscribe to the Home Swapping Circle International and give it at least one try. If they found themselves in a dump in Amsterdam or running from Jack the Ripper in London's back streets, or if they returned to discover their precious home had been vandalised by their guests, they would stop the silly scheme with immediate effect. The only condition Etta managed to ease in edgeways was that they would never, ever take a flight; they'd travel exclusively by train or coach or car.

THEY'D CELEBRATED THEIR FIRST DINNER AS HOUSEMATES AND ETTA was dozing off on her sofa with a full stomach, feeling happy and healthy after the delicious fresh (not frozen) minestrone Dora had prepared.

"Look at that!" cried Dora, her hands clasped on her chest, eyes widened.

"What?" asked Etta, looking at the PC screen that had made Dora as ecstatic as Saint Teresa of Ávila. In response, Dora turned the screen towards her companion.

"Rothenburg ob der Tauber."

"What's that?"

"A small fairy-tale town in the Franconia region of Germany..."

"What's that got to do with anything?"

"We've just received an invitation from a home swap family to stay there. Look what a pretty, beamed old house it is. It has a *biergarten* too."

Etta looked superciliously at the first picture. She had to agree the house looked pretty from the outside.

"Do they show the inside too?"

One by one, Dora showed her the pictures of the cosy home, the old *stube*, the traditional checkered kitchen floor, the geraniums at the windows, the quaint medieval village.

"How are we supposed to get there?"

"By car," said Dora simply. "It's in the southern part of Germany, so not that far. We could stop overnight in Trento where my cousin Angelina lives, and from there it's about five hours' drive."

Travelling through Europe by car? Not a bad idea at all. Etta moved closer to her friend, looking at the pictures again.

"Do you think the house is really as nice as it looks in the pics?"

"Absolutely."

"And what's that?" Etta said, pointing to another picture featuring the city walls and a figure enveloped in a dark cloak, a horn hanging from his neck, a halberd in his hand.

"That's the Rothenburg Watchman giving a night tour of the town."

"Sounds creepy."

"Sounds wonderful! So, should I reply and say we're interested?"

"OK," said Etta, doing her best to sound casual. To maintain her composure, she drew her eyes away from the screen and looked out over her terrace towards the little village perched among the fairy-tale chimney-like rocks, the yellow lamplight making it look almost like a Christmas scene under the full moon.

"What's that?" she cried all of a sudden.

"What's what?" asked Dora, rising from the desk and coming over to join her friend.

"I think I saw a shape moving just under the moon. There – there again!"

"Must be Cassandra flying to say goodbye to her sister, Sibilla."

"Flying? What nonsense!"

∽

Dear Reader,

I hope you enjoyed this mystery. There are three more books coming up featuring Dora and Etta, and new ones to come.

In the meantime...

Is there any way a reader may help an author? Yes! Please **leave a review on Amazon, Goodreads** and/or **Bookbub**. It doesn't matter how long or short it is; even a single sentence can say all that needs to be said. We may live in a digital era, but **this old world of ours still revolves around word of mouth.** A review allows a book to leave the shadows of the unknown and introduces it to other passionate readers.

Grazie :)

THE WATCHMAN OF ROTHENBURG DIES

A GERMAN COZY MYSTERY

The Watchman of Rothenburg Dies is the first book in the
Homeswappers Mystery series.

TO BE RELEASED ON 1 SEPTEMBER 2020

**A bat-like figure slowly unfurls from the darkness – the Night
Watchman is ready for you now.**

Etta and Dora, two newly retired teachers, travel from their home in
Southern Italy to a fairy-tale German town for their first home swap
holiday, delighted to be embraced into the community as soon as they
arrive with an invitation to dinner. But the welcome turns sour when
the Night Watchman of Rothenburg, is brutally murdered while his tour
group takes photographs nearby, a halberd buried in his chest and a
peculiar iron mask by his side.

When the murderer claims a second victim and the son of their
hospitable neighbours becomes the number-one suspect, Etta's

analytical mind goes to work. Why was a shame mask left at the scene of each murder? Is there a clandestine trade going on behind the scenes of apparently upstanding local businesses? And why does every lead take her back to the sinister Devil's Ale pub and the terrifying Rothenburg Barbarossa who lurk within?

Meanwhile, Dora has a puzzle of her own – how to persuade Etta that Sauer's loveably disobedient Basset Hound, Napoleon, is now a permanent part of their lives.

Pack your bags, jump into the backseat of Etta and Dora's ancient car, and join them on their travels around Europe. There'll be mystery, murder and mayhem aplenty wherever they go.

A WEDDING AND A FUNERAL IN MECKLENBURG

A GERMAN COZY MYSTERY

A Wedding and A Funeral, in Mecklenburg is the second book in the *Homeswappers Mystery* series.

TO BE RELEASED ON 15 OCTOBER 2020

Weddings can be Murder

Retired teachers, Etta and Dora, continue their homeswapping adventures across small European towns in their yellow Fiat 500.

Their latest journey leads them to a beautiful mansion in Mecklenburg Pomerania, the Land of a Thousand Lakes in Northern Germany.

Excited at having been invited to their homeswappers' son's wedding, Etta and Dora would never have expected to witness one of the wedding party dropping into the wedding cake... dead!

With the help of Leon, their basset hound, and his heart-melting skills,

Dora's charm and intuition, and Etta's sharp mind, the three sleuths set out on the trail of the murderer.

But does that road lead to grave danger?

[Final Blurb to Come]

AN AERO ISLAND CHRISTMAS MYSTERY

A DANISH COZY MYSTERY

An Aero Island Christmas Mystery is the third book in the
Homeswappers Mystery series.

TO BE RELEASED ON 1 DECEMBER 2020

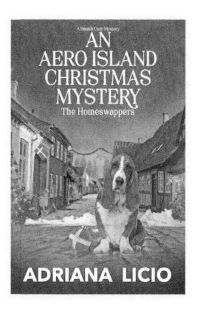

When Dora, Etta and Basset Hound Leon accepted a homeswap
invitation to the Danish Island of Aero for Christmas, they had
imagined cobbled streets sparkling with twinkling lights, holding a hot
cup of mulled wine to warm up, the scent of baked goods hitting their
nostrils, candles on the window sills of cute timbered houses,
experiencing Danish hygge through and through...

... what they hadn't imagined was to stumble in a skeleton in the
mansard of their home.

Found bodies do have a habit of stirring waters, even muddy waters from the past.

Can the usual trio make sure is a happy Christmas on the island or will the cornered killer feel it's time to strike again?

[Final Blurb to Come]

MORE BOOKS FROM ADRIANA LICIO

THE HOMESWAPPERS SERIES
1 - The Watchman of Rothenburg Dies: A German Travel Mystery – coming on 1 September 2020 - Preorder Now
2 - A Wedding and A Funeral in Mecklenburg : A German Cozy Mystery – coming on 15 October 2020 - Preorder Now
3 - An Aero Island Christmas Mystery: A Danish Cozy Mystery – coming on 1 December 2020 - Preorder Now

AN ITALIAN VILLAGE MYSTERY SERIES
0 - And Then There Were Bones. What better than an invitation for a murder mystery week-end on a sunny Calabrian Island? Or maybe not? *And Then There Were Bones* is the prequel to the *An Italian Village Mystery* series, and it is **available for free by signing up to www.adrianalicio.com/murderclub**
1 - Murder on the Road Returning to her quaint hometown in Italy following the collapse of her engagement, feisty travel writer Giò Brando just wants some peace and quiet. Instead, she finds herself a suspect in a brutal murder.
2 A Fair Time for Death is a mystery set during the Autumn Chestnut Fair in Trecchina, a mountain village near Maratea,

involving a perfume with a split personality, a disappearing corpse, a disturbing secret from the past and a mischievous goat.

3 - A Mystery Before Christmas A haunting Christmas song from a faraway land. A child with striking green eyes. A man with no past. A heartwarming mystery for those who want to breathe in the delicious scents and flavours of a Mediterranean December.

4 - Peril at the Pellicano Hotel – A group of wordsmiths, a remote hotel. Outside, the winds howl and the seas rage. But the real danger lurks within.

JOIN THE MARATEA MURDER CLUB

Sign up to my mailing list for exclusive content:

- **Book 0,** *And Then There Were Bones,* the prequel to the *An Italian Village Mystery* series available nowhere else
- **Giò Brando's Maratea Album** – photos of her favourite places and behind-the-scenes secrets
- **A Maratea Map** – including most places featured in the series
- **Adriana Licio's News** – new releases, news from Maratea, but no spam – Etta would loathe it!
- **Cosy Mystery Passion:** a place to share favourite books, characters, tips and tropes

Sign up to **www.adrianalicio.com/murderclub**

AUTHOR'S NOTE

In 2005, Giovanni, my hubby, mentioned that we (both being travel freaks) should join a homeswapping association so we could travel more often and see places in a different light. At the time, I didn't pay much attention. The idea of having 'strangers' wandering about my home held no attraction for me.

But he tried again and again. If I'm stubborn, Giovanni's even more so. He turned up in my perfumery with a friend of his, a teacher from Padova who has literally travelled the world using home exchange schemes. She has two girls, and they have been travelling with their parents since they were babies.

Has she ever found her home disrupted on her return? Never in more than 40 home swaps.

Has she made new friends? Plenty.

Doesn't she find hotels are more comfortable? No, they are less personal. She has come to loathe the very idea of spending her holidays in a hotel.

The next day, I called Annalisa, an amazing woman and the President of the Italian branch of an international home swap organisation. She had organised something like 150 successful home swaps, and by then had a real sense of belonging to the world. Her two children had been brought up by countless different families, because yes, you can also swap children if you're fed up with your own...

OK, I'm kidding, but under the scheme, you can host a family's child, and then have the favour returned.

With home swapping, for a weekend, a week, a month, you don't spend a small fortune to stay in an anonymous hotel with thousands of other tourists; you become part of the local community, staying in a family house that's typical of the area. You use their bikes (or kayaks), you're given directions to the local markets, the best bakeries, the most exciting activities in town, the tiny restaurants that never make it into a tourist guide. And more often than not, you get invited for a cup of coffee, an aperitivo or even dinner with your new neighbours (who have been duly informed by your hosts).

Two months after my talk with Annalisa, we were staying in a splendid riad in the Marrakech Medina. We have travelled to Vancouver Island, Berlin, London, Hamelin (the town of the Pied Piper), and then in 2009, Frodo, our adventurous golden retriever, joined the family. To my utmost surprise, we've never had to house the jolly beastie in dog care while we take a holiday. We just gave up flights and started to drive all the way from down, down, down the Italian boot to Sweden, Great Britain, Switzerland, Brittany, Slovakia, the Pyrenees and many more places.

It's now 2020 and the Coronavirus pandemic is sweeping the globe. This will be the first year since 2005 that we won't house swap with anyone, so I've handed the baton to Etta and Dora and am enjoying my armchair travels as much as I hope my readers will. And this is only temporary; I'm waiting for the day we'll be able to hit the road again.

About witches

Witches are a strong part of Italian folklore, especially in the South. In times when doctors were mainly a luxury for the rich, ordinary people used to go to the local witches for all their troubles, without making any great distinction between health conditions and human emotions, hence the requests for love potions, the evil eye, protection of the soldiers abroad etc.

The Path of the Seven Stones really exists. It is what we call a 'literary walk', illustrating the story of Vito and the Witch as described by Mimmo Sammartino in his book *Vito Ballava con le Streghe*. This short tale is based on the legend that Dora tells Etta, which is just one version amongst the many different ones spread all over Southern Italy. In some, the husband doesn't break the jar, but substitutes common water for the oil, and the witch doesn't die but 'simply' breaks her legs, her husband saying triumphantly that "it's better to have a wife with broken legs than a healthy witch." Of all the variations, I much prefer Mimmo Sammartino's for its drama, the tragedy of the man discovering too late that his wife may have been a witch, but she really loved him, and he loved her passionately in return.

The walk goes from the village of Castelmezzano to Pietrapertosa with seven stops along the way, each marked with a stone sculpture representing the main points of the story. The stop at the Witches' Cave is called the Flight, and nearby are a giant oak tree, some ruins and the reproduction of an ancient mosaic featuring the Witches' Dance.

ABOUT THE AUTHOR

Adriana Licio lives in the Apennine Mountains in southern Italy, not far from Maratea, the seaside setting for her first cosy series, *An Italian Village Mystery*.

She loves loads of things: travelling, reading, walking, good food, small villages, and homeswapping. A long time ago, she spent six years falling in love with Scotland, and she has never recovered. She now runs her family perfumery, and between a dark patchouli and a musky rose, she devours cosy mysteries.

She resisted writing as long as she could, fearing she might get carried away by her fertile imagination. But one day, she found an alluring blank page and the words flowed in the weird English she'd learned in Glasgow.

Adriana finds peace for her restless, enthusiastic soul by walking in nature with her adventurous golden retriever Frodo and her hubby Giovanni.

Do you want to know more?
Join the **Maratea Murder Club**

You can also stay in touch on:
www.adrianalicio.com

facebook.com/adrianalicio.mystery

twitter.com/adrianalici

amazon.com/author/adrianalicio

bookbub.com/authors/adriana-licio

GLOSSARY

NATALE – Christmas in Italian. Traditionally, the name was given to babies, both males and females, born on 25 December.

ORECCHIETTE – literally, this means 'small ears'. This pasta is skilfully shaped with a knife, then on the tip of your thumb to look like a small ear. If you want to have fun, google 'fare le orecchiette Pugliesi' and enjoy the videos showing how skilful and fast the real pasta makers can be.

PASSOLINA – this was a name my mother gave to raisins. In Italian, they are called 'uva passa', and 'passolina' would literally mean small uva passa, but this is far from obvious to anyone except members of my family. In fact, I remember as a child, I was despatched to fetch a bag of raisins from the local food store, as they're the ingredients for both chicories and meat rolls. Stefano, the food store owner, never ready to give up on a sale easily, kept asking me over and over again what it was that I had been sent to buy, and I was totally unable to explain what the small, sweet things were as I only knew them as 'passoline'. In the end, I had to go back home and ask for the correct name. That was my first experience of speaking a foreign language.

PEPE – pepper

RABATANA – this has origins in the Arabian word *rabhàdi* (meaning a small suburb). Arabs lived in this area throughout the IX and X century, Pietrapertosa being a strategic stronghold as it was difficult to access, while the view spanned all around towards the Basento River, from which potential assailants might be coming. Around the stronghold, a small settlement sprang up. Farmers and traders built their tiny houses, perched atop the mountains, and connecting the whole lot of them is a maze of tiny alleys that still form the Rabatana quarter of the village.

RUCOLA – rocket salad

SPECK – smoked cured ham

Printed in Great Britain
by Amazon